W9-BPK-111

The

Madonna

Stories

Other books by Gary Paulsen
published by Harcourt Brace & Company

Clabbered Dirt, Sweet Grass
Eastern Sun, Winter Moon

FOR CHILDREN

Harris and Me
Sisters/Hermanas

GARY PAULSEN

The

Madonna

Stories

A HARVEST BOOK

HARCOURT BRACE & COMPANY

San Diego   New York   London

Copyright © 1989 by Gary Paulsen

All rights reserved.
No part of this publication may be
reproduced or transmitted in any form or by any means,
electronic or mechanical, including photocopy, recording, or
any information storage and retrieval system, without
permission in writing from the publisher.

Requests for permission to make copies
of any part of the work should be mailed to:
Permissions Department,
Harcourt Brace & Company, 8th Floor,
Orlando, Florida 32887.

"The Library" first appeared in *The Loon Feather*.

Library of Congress Catalog Card Number: 89-50059

Printed in the United States of America

First Harvest Edition 1993

A B C D E

This book is dedicated
to Ruth

Contents

The Madonna

I N THAT TIME, when there was only the insanity of the incoming shells, day after day, hour after hour, in that time when they came in while he sat in the bunkers and he smelled the damp mud sand in the bags around him and felt the tight jolts as they hit, in that time was when he started to drink.

He knew that.

In that time, when he was beyond life into death, he started to drink, and to drink more to make it end.

But, of course, it didn't end. Not until they finally tore him enough so that he was sent back to the world, The World, and by then he was too good at drinking to stop.

He knew that. He knew when he started to drink. It was in that time. And then they sent him back and let him go in California, let him go back into The World, but he was not one of those who could kill himself, so he kept to drinking and left California and went to a small town in New Mexico. He could live cheaply there, he had heard.

And it wasn't too bad. At first there had been some fighting because they thought he was a hippy. But when he didn't fight back and only wanted to drink, when he didn't talk back and only wanted to drink, when he did nothing back but only wanted to drink, they at first laughed and then took pity on him and then they left him alone. Or perhaps it wasn't pity, but he felt it to be that and, since they left him alone, that was all that counted. To be left alone in Taos, New Mexico, drunk, was all that counted for him and, he thought, all that counted for everyone.

Until it was given to him to deliver the Christ.

When he could think clearly, or more clearly than at other times, that was how he thought of it: deliver the Christ. And often when he awakened in the mornings, or came up to find the bottle next to the bed, he would fight to remember just how it had happened.

It wasn't much of a fight, the fight to remember, but he stayed with it until he got a headache and the feeling from the bottle would come in, and for just the briefest time he could see it all as it happened.

Or as he thought it had happened.

That night had started as they almost always started when he got the check they sent him for breaking him—he called it his 'repair check'. They sent him the check each month, and when he got it he would go to the cantina on the plaza and try to shoot pool. He would buy drinks for everyone until the check was gone. Then they would buy drinks for him until he was too finished to drink more, and he would leave.

Out, across the plaza, he would walk until he found

the small street that led back to the room he rented where he could fall back into the damp nest of his bed and end that day.

And this night was much of that, except that he tried to get Sara to dance with him before he left. Sara painted signs and was fun to watch when she danced, but she said he was too drunk. Yet she said it in a way that made him happy, a smiling way, so he left across the plaza that night in a happy mood. And because of that he decided to visit Kit Carson's grave—in an old graveyard behind the hotel—and think about being happy.

And because he was happy and decided to stop and think at Kit's grave, he was the one who got to deliver the Christ.

Or that's how he remembered it.

It was a scream that stopped him and made him crouch down until he fell.

He was in the alley near the back of the hotel, not too far from the grave, when he heard the scream. It started high, a pain scream—he had heard many of those, and knew them well—and it faded off into chunks of sound mixed with breath and spit that he also knew well.

At first he thought something had happened and he was back in The Country and fell to the ground for that, to hide from the snapping death that seemed to have always come with the screams. But even drunk he knew that that wasn't true, so he stood again. There was only silence for a time. He began to think he dreamed the whole thing—he had many dreams while walking—but another sound followed the scream and he knew it was a woman and that she needed help.

He had also heard that sound before, but did not like to think about it.

In a few steps he realized that the sound was coming from Kit Carson's grave, or near it, and he moved that way. He thought perhaps it was a woman being raped. But when he got to the grave he saw a young woman alone, lying on her back near the grave, her hands pulling at the small fence surrounding the grave.

"Help me," she said, or he thought she said. She might have thought it and he got it from the bend in her body. "Help me now."

She was pregnant, huge with it, and still he did not understand.

"I don't know what to do," he answered. "What is the matter?"

His words doubled on him in his mind with the drink, and everything echoed.

"It's time. Help me."

So, he thought. *She means the baby.*

"There is nothing I can do." He meant it literally. There was nothing he could do. He would have stopped it for her, but he could not do it. He could do nothing. It always seemed in all things that he could do nothing.

"Please," she said. A tiny sound. *Please.*

And there it was. They always said it when there was nothing you could do. They always said *please* in a small voice.

He kneeled next to her and put his hands in his lap and waited. He had done that before. He had sat next to them and waited when they made the small sounds, waited for them to die, and he thought that was coming now. He knew of that.

But instead of dying she screamed and heaved,

great doublings of her stomach, great heaves. They were of pain, but they were more, too. The heaves came from inside her, from the earth beneath her, and from something he did not understand or know. The heaves took him back farther, back to when he had kneeled next to another person who had heaved.

She screamed again, and the scream went into his thoughts and mixed with the memory and he was not there, not at Kit Carson's grave watching the hippy girl have a baby, but back more, back where he started to drink, back where Wendell was leaning against a tree holding his stomach in with the heaves coming. Wendell who was dying, who had said *please* in a small voice when he could not stop it.

He went back to that and the girl heaved again. Tightened and heaved and her dress rode up and the head came, but he did not see it as a head. He saw instead Wendell's coil, and he thought that was it, thought that it was the same, and he reached down to push it back in as he had done with Wendell. But she heaved again and the baby slid out on the ground, slid out between her legs in blood and placenta, slid out before he could push it back.

It all mixed in his mind, Wendell and the grey coil and the short pain sounds and the head of the baby. He reached down and picked the baby up and put it on the girl's stomach as tenderly as he had picked up Wendell's coil and placed it on the dying man's stomach.

That's when she looked at him and smiled and said, "Christ."

And he thought, *Of course, it's Christ.*

That was how he came to meet the Madonna and deliver the Christ. But he left her there, left her and went home.

Nights later he went to the cantina and tried to tell the man at the bar that he had delivered the second Christ, but the man moved away.

That was the way of it, he thought. When he talked of the incoming insanity, they thought much of it and bought him drinks to hear of that time. But when something important like the Christ came along, they moved away.

He knew that it would never happen again. Many

nights, after drinking in the cantina, he would go out across the plaza, through the other drunk men in their blankets, and he would sit near the fountain. He would sit near the fountain and cry because he'd met the Madonna. He had met her and delivered the Christ, and it had changed nothing for him.

When the crying was finished he would sit and try to think about it. But all that would come would be the memory of it, the nudge of wonder about what she was doing now, the Madonna and the little Christ she had.

Then he would go back into the cantina, if they would let him, and drink some more and watch the artists shoot pool in the back room, and he would tell the stories about the incoming explosions for the drinks that they would buy him.

The Cook Camp

DURING THE SECOND World War the boy's father fought across Europe and took a French nurse as a mistress. And while he had much to tell in the letters he wrote of fighting Germans and the War, he had nothing to say of the nurse. But this is not a story about the boy's father except to balance the other part. The part about the cook camp.

He was a small boy, and there was great excitement in the land if you were a small boy in the time of war. He did not understand the horror of it, but thought of it as a game. A grand game against Krauts and Nips, and he turned the South Side Chicago apartment into a tiny war and fought as well as he could with a wooden rifle and a fiber helmet liner. His mother worked in a war plant, making twenty millimeter ammunition. Sometimes she would bring home empty casings, which he pretended had been fired at the enemy, and that could have gone on and on for a small boy in that time of killing.

But a day came when his mother brought a man home. He was a large man with short blond hair and wide shoulders and a broad smile. The boy liked him at once and when his mother told him that he must call the man uncle, the boy thought it strange that he had not met this uncle before.

"He is your uncle Casey," she said, "and he will be living with us for a little while."

The uncle and the boy's mother slept on the couch while the boy slept in the one small bedroom. At night when they thought he was asleep they made noises that the boy did not understand. He would lie awake in the semi-darkness watching the blue neon light flash outside and hear the noises and not know why he felt bad. When he asked his mother why he felt bad, her face went white and she held him and began to cry.

"You have to stay with your grandmother for a while," she said. "It's this war—this damn war."

The boy knew it wasn't the war. He knew it was Casey.

He was sent to northern Minnesota to stay with his grandmother in a cook camp for a road crew that was cutting a road through the woods into Canada. His mother put him on a train in Chicago with a note pinned to his jacket, and he rode trains for a day and a night and part of another day, and when it stopped his grandmother was waiting at the depot.

His grandmother was from the old country. She had come and homesteaded and raised nine children before her husband died. When she came to the time for living alone she had no money and had to work doing what she did best, cooking. At first she cooked in the lumber camps, but after a while the camps died off and she went to work in a series of small cafés. Then the small towns slowly collapsed and the cafés thinned and went down, and she took work at last in the cook camp.

She was a small, thin woman, with a great braid of hair she kept in a bun. And she would let her hair down before bed, down past her waist. At night in the cook trailer, where they slept on two bunks near the stove, she would comb her hair with a coarse-tooth comb and sing Norwegian songs in the yellow light from the oil lamp on the table.

Sometimes in the night the boy would awaken, crying, thinking of Chicago and missing his mother. Then his grandmother would hold him and cut a piece of apple pie. And sometimes the boy may have cried more for the pie than for his mother, there in the cook camp on the edge of the woods.

The camp was a raw place, raw and hard. The men who drove the Cats and the gravel trucks were all huge. They would come in to eat smelling of diesel fuel and oil and tobacco, which they spat in a can by the door. But they all took their hats off and ruffled the boy's hair. And they were always polite and gentle with his grandmother as they thanked her for the food. The boy had never seen men eat as they ate. He stared at the great heaps of meat and potatoes they devoured until his grandmother told him it was wrong to stare and he stopped.

One morning, just after the men had left the cook trailer, there was a deep bellow and they carried a man back in and put him on the table.

A tree had backed on the man, come back down across the Cat he'd been driving. A limb had come through the protective pipes welded over the driver's seat and it caught his elbow on the armrest and crushed it. When they laid the man on the table, he started to go into shock. The man's face went white and his nostrils pinched and there was saliva at the corners of his mouth. The boy's grandmother made a clucking sound as some of the men held his feet up and the color returned and the pain came up. He lay that way, grunting in pain while she taped his elbow to a board so they could take him to a doctor, some sixty rough miles away.

When they had taken the man away she wiped the table with hot water and soap.

"It isn't only the war that hurts." She said it to herself, scrubbing hard while the boy watched. She was crying, soft tears down her cheeks, crying as she scrubbed. And when she saw the boy looking, she turned away but kept scrubbing until the table was clean. Then they sat down and had some apple pie.

There came a night when the boy awakened crying and his grandmother asked him what was bothering him. She sat in the yellow glow from the lamp on the table in back, the light coming around her head, and the boy sat in her lap and told her about uncle Casey. He asked her why he felt bad about the noises and he felt her stiffen, but she said nothing. She only held him closer, tighter, and rocked with him until he went back to sleep and he would not have known more of what she thought except for the flies.

During the summer days the flies would come in, and she hated them. She hated them personally and deeply and she killed them with a small screen swatter which she used with tiny, deadly flicks of her wrist. The flies became the problems, they became the boy's father in Europe and the worry of that, and they became the boy's mother and Chicago and all of it.

A letter came for his grandmother, brought in by a dirty-faced man who drove a gravel truck, and he handed her the letter and said that it was from Europe and spat in the can by the door as he left. It was not bad news, except that it was from the boy's father and he was fighting and that frightened her. But it caused her to think, to see too many things.

When she was finished with the letter she sat and cried for a time. The boy went to her and held her hand but he could not help, and after a while she stood and took the swatter and began to kill flies. With little death-flicks, little cuts in the air, she dropped them on the table and brushed them onto the floor with the swatter. The boy went to the stove and watched her flick them and cry, and once she turned, just once, and her eyes were burning and she said to no one, not even herself, "Damn this war and the damn cities and the damned men. . . ."

"What men?" the boy asked.

But it was gone, the edged sound was gone then and she went on killing the flies, taking them down, until they were all dead. Then she cut apple pie and the two of them sat and ate in silence, sat in the cook camp where they were building the roads into Canada.

Sex

T HE SECOND WOMAN was best.

Although there were other women after that, other women and three wives, he was sure the second woman was best.

He came from youth, from the hot swollen thickness of youth through the first, feeble gropings which somehow never went well; he tried to change but could not, and one day he walked into a church just to look at the stained glass windows and the second woman was there.

She was a brunette with blue-green eyes. She was tall and did not wear a bra and moved easily when she walked, and when she smiled at him he did not know how things would be later, so he smiled back and there it was.

There they were.

There would be other lives later, and marriages and divorces and many changes but they did not know that then, did not know they were really for other people, so they bought an old Buick and traveled. They drove around the West in the old car and taught each other about sex.

Of course they called it love and said it all the time and pretended great affection for each other and made all the sounds of undying love they were taught to make by movies and books and ministers and families, but it was not. They moaned of love and

listened to songs of love and cried of love and screamed of love. Their ignorance was the sum of two igno-
rances multiplied rather than added, the ignorance
of sex that thinks it is love.

Hot, wet, sweet, moving, thrusting, pulling, holding, throbbing, screaming, touching, gasping love.

That is what they had, and he thought it was
the best.

They called it making love, and to be sure it was
better than making hate. There were bumper stickers
then that called it making love. Make Love, Not War,
the stickers said. Love. They did not say have sex not
war, or make sex not war, or make physical attraction
not war, or get together not war, or even lust not war,
and so naturally they thought they had love and he
probably would never have known different because
he was from a time and place where you had great
faithfulness to what you thought you loved, even if it
was wrong.

In his youth, when he was sure that he was ugly,
knew he was ugly, he dreamed that if he ever found
a woman who would take him, to be with him, to stay
with him, he would never do anything to make her

leave and so he would never have known the truth. He would have spent his life calling it love and loving it, the thing with the traveling woman, but she saw it first, saw their mistake, and she told him without knowing she was telling him.

It was that she hurt him—that was how he found out—she hurt him so badly that he never recovered and she did not even know she had hurt him.

He thought it was love and yearned for the magic of it, the mystical part of love that seemed to come from soft light and breath that mixed. He wished it to be so much that he thought it was there.

When they made love he worshipped it, lived for it, and made more of it than it could possibly be for anybody, more than it would be for the woman.

They traveled, driving through Utah and Arizona, and they finally came to New Mexico, to a place where the Rio Grande is held back by a dam at a place called Elephant Butte. Below the dam the river is no more than a trickle, but they had been driving all day and they needed to rest, so they turned off on a dirt trail and by chance came to what he thought was the most beautiful place in the whole world: a small clearing in the tall cottonwoods next to the muddy stream that was the Rio Grande. They set up camp in the dark and he made a fire of dry dead cottonwood. Then they spread out their sleeping bag, crawled inside, and made love.

But inside he felt different this time, as though being within her were almost holy. He felt that it was too wonderful, too rich, and too much of love.

Then they slept.

In the night the spillway of the dam was opened and at first dawn, when the sun was just showing above the buttes to the east, he opened his eyes and where there had been a muddy trickle, there was now a river.

It filled the banks, flowing quietly, and it brought gold down on them. His eyes opened and the shaft of gold from the top curve of the sun came across the water in a golden ray, a ray of light that came through the fine, soft hairs in front of her temples, still moist from making love, so that the gold from the sun mixed with the gold from the river and the gold from the soft after-love hairs and came into him, into and of him and there was all the love in the world there.

Right there, from the sun and soft hairs, was all the love in the world to be had by anybody, and he pulled the bag back so she lay naked and sleeping in the light. He looked at her body as she slept in the early light. He looked at her breasts and nipples, cold and hard in the gold light, and at her stomach rising slightly, and at her fine legs. He looked again at the soft hair at her temples and he thought: I love you now and will love you until I die and there is only love, only love in the whole world, only our love, and then she opened her eyes.

"What a wonderful hump that was," she said, only she did not use that word but another one, and then she went on to say it again in different ways, as if she liked speaking of it crudely, as if she thought he would like it referred to that way as well. She spoke of it as if it had been a bodily function, a release, but it was too glaring, too much a difference from what he thought it was. It seared into his thoughts, cut away the romance, brought ugliness in where he thought it simply could not be, could not really be.

He tried to tell her of the golden light and the sun and the joy he felt, but she put her hand on him then, and it was over. The grandness, the mist of it was gone and it would not come again with the second woman.

The Killing Chute

As a boy he worked for a man who cut meat. The man's business was in an old building in the northwest corner of Minnesota and was a locker plant, on a tiny basis. The man had a walk-in cooler and a meat-cutting room with tables and grinders and a bandsaw and a large wife.

He put his wife in that way, as a piece of equipment. That is how the man thought of it, as his father, and his father's father had thought of it: to have a cooler and tables and grinders and a bandsaw and a large wife.

The man's wife was named Clara and she was stout but not fat, well-framed and strong. She wore her brown hair tied back except for some loose strands that always hung down to the side. She would push back her hair with the inside of her arm where there wasn't any blood or dirt. The wrist and hand had great beauty when they pushed the hair back, a kind of curving beauty and flow that sometimes caught the boy's glance and he would stare. In this way, the woman's softness came from her wrist to his eye and it was from Clara that beauty came here at all, curled in her graceful hand, in her touch, even amidst death.

At the back of the old building there was a wooden chute set about three feet off the ground, so that live animals could be unloaded directly from the bed of a truck. The chute led into the building through a door that swung in and slammed shut behind each animal.

Once the animal was through the door and the door

closed to its rear, it could not move; the pig or steer or sheep found itself in a welded-pipe enclosure in a concrete room with a drain in the floor and water running all the time. The animal stood on a raised platform, and there it would die.

The man would walk up to the animal and put a small gun, a cheap small .22 rifle to the animal's forehead, to a place where an imaginary X crossed from each ear to eye, and he would pull the trigger. The animal would take the bullet from the cheap little gun and slump to its knees and the man would quickly cut its throat while his wife would catch the blood in a pan to make sausage. Stunned by the bullet and bled out by the sharp knife, the animal would die and void itself into the running drain before being hauled up and out and cut into meat.

There is much talk of dumb animals, but of course they are not, not dumb at all, and in some ways are much smarter than humans. The animals that were brought to the chute from small farms or pens, the animals that had been raised and petted and babied and held, these animals were the least stupid of all. The people who owned them could not kill them, so they brought them to the locker plant, to the killing chute. These animals learned in betrayal, knew in betrayal, had infinite knowledge in betrayal.

And if there were mercy the animals would not know what was going to happen, could not know, but there isn't mercy, and so there is the smell. The death smell. The smell of blood and heat and dirt and urine and feces mixed into all things, the smell that fills armies and slaughter plants. The animals knew when they came into the chute, when they smelled the death smell, knew then that they were to die.

They would look stunned, dazed, sadly lost in this final, devastating betrayal, and in that moment before the bullet entered their brain and they slumped to be cut, in that sad, endless moment, the woman would reach out her hand and touch them because she could not stand it. The boy would watch her touch the steers and pigs and sheep and give them some softness, some gentleness to die with, to take with them, some soft part of the world to take.

When the boy had grown to be a young man it was no longer possible for him to visit the room without thinking of horror, of death camps and genocide and clinical killing and My Lai and Cambodia. And it was no longer possible to see the room without thinking of the other death, the human death, the cancer death of his friend.

And so to cancer.

It came to his friend with a small cheap backache that lingered, almost not there until one morning he awakened and his legs would not move correctly, had a numbness, and the doctors told him he had a tumor in his spine that had spread throughout his body, and he could not live.

He could want to live and wish to live and dream to live and hope to live and pray to live and cry to live, but there isn't mercy, and he could not live. The tumor was eating him and would soon eat his brain, and then what he was would end.

It was given to his friend to die in a concrete room on the seventh floor of a hospital in Milwaukee in his fifty-first year, the same year that his business became successful, and he became rich and fulfilled. And there was no dignity—just as there is no mercy—because he had lost control of his bowels, and it either ran from him onto the sheets or became too hard from the constant drip of the painkiller and they had to pick it out of him with gloved fingers.

They.

The nurses.

There were many in the time that took him to the end, but one of them became a part of the memory of women and the memory of death in the boy who had become the young man, the boy from the killing chute. This nurse was blonde and large, and she had smiles for the dying man, she was smiles for him, and her name was Anna.

Once, when the young man could not stand it, could not stand to be in the room, he went out to the hall to cry and to look out at the gray of Milwaukee, the wide gray of Milwaukee where it would all end soon. And when he came back into the room, Anna was sitting on the edge of the bed with the man who was dying.

He was telling her something, explaining something intensely, importantly, as all things had become intense and important in the magnification of death. He fought to speak through the drugs, and when the young man drew close he realized it was a story about the first time his friend had made love.

But he was too addled to tell it correctly. He forgot the date and time and place and even the woman, mixed it all up in the drug-speak, but Anna sat quietly. She held his hand, and her wrist, the sweet curve of her arm, took the young man back to Clara and the killing chute. Anna reached out her hand, the final blessing, the sweetness and grace to help through the final betrayal. She meant the smile and she meant the curve of her wrist and hand into his wrist and hand; she meant the softness and the compassion, and when he went under with the drugs, as the new load hit him, Anna turned to the young man and smiled sadly.

"He is very smart," she said.

"The smartest man I have ever known," the young man answered, as though it had been a question.

"Many of the men like to talk about it, their first time. Women almost always talk about their children and men talk about their first time."

"He didn't have children. Doesn't, I mean. He doesn't have children."

"Even so. Men talk about their first time. Even when they have children. Sometimes they touch me, you know, here, and here, and I let them. It doesn't mean anything and their voices are so. . . so small. But I can tell he is smart, the way he uses words."

But all he could think of was the curve of her wrist and hand as she held the thin hand of the man in the bed, the dying hand of the man in the bed. It was the same hand she had used to clean him out, to clean the sheets, to help him, to grace him, to death him. It was the same beautiful hand and wrist from the killing chute to the hospital bed, and he sat on the edge of the bed with the nurse to wait for his friend to die, waiting as he had waited by the killing chute when he was a boy.

Rape

BECAUSE HE BELIEVED the lies about becoming a man, he found himself in that ultimate lie about manhood—that he should seek danger to prove he was a man—and he sought to put himself in harm's way and that brought him, finally, to understand rape, or the edges of it.

The harm he sought was in Mexico. It was possible to find harm in many places, but he went to
Mexico because he had heard it was easy to find there
and did not cost so much.

But it worked too well; harm came too easily.

He was in a small bar, a cheap dirty stinking little
place in Mexico where it was possible to get two shots
of tequila for a nickel, served in a grimy glass—a dollar
for forty shots of a drink that would turn your brain to
liquid. He was drunk when a Mexican policeman
came in. In his drunkenness, he shouted something
stupid to the cop and found himself looking down the
top of the barrel of a chrome-plated .45 automatic
which had been jammed in his left nostril.

Death was close then and he knew it. The policeman did not care if he lived or died—it made no difference at all to him, and that was in his eyes. With
the barrel of the gun still in his nose he was backed out
of the bar, put in an old Dodge police car, and taken
to the Mexican jail where he spent one night.

One night.

One night in a fenced-in enclosure they called
"the pit". Other men were there, many of them, and

in that night in the pit some of the men decided to rape him.

They said nothing but several of them touched him as they shouldn't have and though he knocked their hands away they persisted and he retreated to a corner of the fence. Outside the wire the guards laughed and joked and pointed with their chins and money was bet on him and overhead a bare light bulb made the room a white he would never be able to stand again and four of the men came for him.

At first he did not believe it, could not believe that the police were betting on it and would not stop it. He fought them off, half-expecting it to be a joke, fought them off as he could. But they were silent, the four, and they kept coming and when one of them positioned himself between his legs, he went mad with the fear of it. He fought like an animal, biting and kicking and screaming until the heels of his boots were red with blood and they at last left him alone.

He crouched panting in the corner. Taking short chokes of air, never enough air, he watched them the rest of that long night, his whole-life-night in the white light from the white bulb in the ceiling. Then he knew some of harm and some of rape, but he would not know more until he saw the other side of it.

The other side of rape.

After he got out of jail, he spent two days drinking in a cheap hotel. He heard that some soldiers were going to go back into the hills in the long canyons from Chihuahua to the coast. There was a band of insurgents there—*banditos*—and they were to be taken. He told the soldiers that he was a Yankee reporter and they agreed to let him go with them.

He found the troop cars in the switching yards of the station and climbed on with a small bag and a bottle of tequila.

They traveled in troop cars attached to a passenger train, but the soldiers quickly moved from the troop car to the club car, getting louder and more ridiculous as soldiers. Some of them carried two rifles, crossed over their backs with the slings across their fronts and they postured and blustered up and down the train like children at dangerous play.

The train passed through little villages along the way, never going very fast. At some of the villages the train would stop to pick up passengers. Boys would

come onto the train at these stops with buckets full of
dark Mexican beer and burritos which they sold as
they ran through the cars. After several villages, he
found himself sitting in the observation car with one
of the soldiers, a chunky man who spoke broken
English, and they shared a bottle of tequila with the
false sense of camaraderie that comes from drinking.

Sitting directly in front of them were two young
American women with straw hats on. The women
were angry about the stops and the soldiers and the
train. They spoke loudly, criticizing everything
Mexican.

As the train came to a stop in a village, he looked
out of the window and he saw a woman in a full skirt
and peasant blouse squat suddenly, raise her skirt and
push a handful of sand up between her legs.

It was so sudden that he made a sound of surprise
and the Mexican soldier looked out and saw it and
laughed harshly.

"She must be from one of the villages back in the
hills," the soldier said. "Back there when they see
soldiers or troop cars they put sand into themselves.
They think it will keep them from being mounted."

Mounted, he thought. Being mounted. He remembered the night in jail and the four men. There
was nothing to say then and he reached for the bottle,
but as he glanced at the Mexican soldier he saw that
the man was watching the two loud American women
in front of him, smiling quietly and studying them and
the way their hair shone in the light coming through
the windows in the top of the train. He knew that it
was the same look he had seen from the men in the
jail, just before they had come for him.

The Grotto

TIME passes.

There is time given to be young, and perhaps stupid, and then older for a time and perhaps still stupid and then it is done—or it is thought to be done.

But the time that passes is different for everyone, and for one man, for this one old man, it passed without stupidity and with some joy, and came in the end to a moment that he took through his last days and into his death.

When he came to be old, he received the warning signals—the small aches, the chest pains, the weight that would not go away—but he chose to go without doctors.

He was deliberate in his choice, studied in it. And it is possible that the doctors could not have helped, but he would not know.

He had a great, wonderful life, with family and success and money. But there was more he needed to do, more he wanted to see.

One of his daughters married a man who owned a sailboat. The son-in-law loved the man more than a father, was closer in many ways, and as things moved to a close, to an end, to when the pains would make his decision not to see doctors so much more important, the two men decided to take the boat out on Lake Powell.

The lake had once been canyons of high red sandstone walls, long winding canyons drowned when the Glenn Canyon dam was built across the Colorado River.

The canyons still held silent beauty, soft-sweeping beauty, where the men could take two weeks to be alone and talk.

It became part of them, the beauty, the red cliffs rising sharply above the boat, catching the sun and blue sky and exploding the colors down to them and on them and in them so that in a while they could not even speak of the beauty any longer. It was the Navajo prayer: beauty above and below and to the left and to the right and to the front and to the rear and all around, beauty.

There was no wind, so they motored for a whole day, moving northeast into the lake. When they had gone many miles up the lake, past countless canyons, they took a side canyon at random. They followed the canyon slowly until it narrowed to two smooth walls that seemed to rise straight up from the sides of the boat and close out the sky until it was only a fine blue line above darkened cathedral walls high above them, high above the mast.

Just when they thought they could go no further, the canyon opened into a small grotto. A blue-green light came down the walls and up through the water so that it seemed to glow. And on the side of the grotto, high up, there was an old cliff dwelling, protected by an overhang.

It was easy to see why a man had made his shelter there. It could not be reached except by footholds chiseled into the rock, small holes softened by a thousand years of wind.

Around the edges of the grotto were smaller pools carved by the same long wind, the old wind that still came each evening as it had for all time, came up the canyons and rubbed gently against the sandstone walls and made sounds of beauty to match the light that came up through the water.

A thousand years, the younger man thought, a thousand years ago a man sat up in the dwelling and looked down on his garden, his rows of corn and thought he would never need another thing. A thousand years and he had had a woman and a child, and it could be seen above the dwelling. On the overhanging rock there was a drawing, a pictograph showing the stick figures of a man and a woman holding a child. It showed stalks of corn and it showed arrows flying from a stick bow held by the stick man, the arrows chasing two other stick men away from the corn.

A thousand years ago a man had pride and triumph and a woman and a child and power and corn and life and all of it was still there in the drawing, still alive in the pictograph. The two men tied the boat to a scrub of brush and settled in to do nothing.

But the older man was restless and wanted other things. He had a seeking thing in him and he wanted to climb the footholds to see the dwelling closer.

The younger man worried about the pains in the old man's chest, but the old man would have none of it. The old man took the rubber dinghy, paddled to where the footholds came out of the water, and he started up. The younger man went with him, but the old man went up first. For a moment the chest pains came and the old man had to stop and hang in the small holes, hang and grimace with the pain, but at last the men reached the dwelling and looked at the remains of the hut. It was six by eight with walls of rocks piled up without a roof. There were bits of a broken pot and the drawing overhead, crudely cut into the sandstone. They sat in silence for a time and then went back down to the boat where it floated in the grotto like some toy caught in a bowl.

And that is where night caught them.

It was hot after dark. They didn't talk, but they ate from a can heated over an alcohol stove. And they sat. The younger man sat in the cockpit and tried to feel what it might have been like years ago to shoot two arrows at the men who would steal your corn, while the older man sat below at the table and read from a book about healing.

No insects came to the light from the battery lamps in the boat. When it grew late, they each took their bunk and fell asleep to the sounds of night birds calling in the grotto.

Morning came as bright sun somewhere, but no direct rays came down into the grotto. The younger man awakened coughing because he smoked, and in his coughing he saw that the older man was gone from his bunk. He brought his feet to the floor and pumped the stove to heat water for instant coffee, then stood to find the older man.

For a moment he worried, thinking the old man had fallen overboard during the night and drowned, but then he saw him.

The older man was in one of the stone pools. It was twice as big as a bathtub with rounded edges and a curved bottom. He was bathing, or starting to, standing naked in the bright morning light with a towel next to him on the rock and a bar of soap in his hand. The younger man started to call, but saw that something was different. He knew that it wasn't just a bath.

On the boat the stove gently whooshed and the pan of water started to heat, but the younger man simply stood and watched the older man. He stood and watched in silence across the water, across the green light, across time, across a thousand years. He watched a bath of light and life.

The old man's dying body sagged where older

men sag, where the younger man was starting to sag. His stomach and chest had lost their tone and hung pale and loose. The skin at the old man's waist and the inside of his thighs where they met the water hung loose. And the belly which had been contained in clothes hung out now and his penis hung into the cold water.

It was a bath across light and time. A bath of life. The old man began his bath as the water on the stove reached temperature. And as the water began to boil on the stove, the younger man could not break his gaze. He stayed watching, looking out from the cabin of the boat. Looking out at the old man's bath.

He saw the old man soap first his face, then rinse it, then soap his hair and rinse it. The old man washed inside his ears and between his fingers and under his arms and in the seam of his elbows. He rubbed the soap smoothly, evenly against his skin, rinsing each part of his body carefully to wash away all the soap before moving on to the next, and then, finally, he washed his penis. He moved it, cleaned it, rinsed it, and then he stood in the green water and looked up at the slice of sky where the blue light met the green light of the water, looked up at the light and the younger man knew then, knew that it was a prayer. A prayer across time and light and water, just as it had been a bath across time and light and water, as the man in the dwelling must have prayed. He knew that it would be the last bath the old man took, the last bath that meant anything to him, and the last prayer he took. There would be no talk, no more talk about what was coming. There would only be the bath.

It was the beginning for the old man. The younger man knew that if he'd had a sharp rock and more time, the old man would have climbed up under the over-hang and carved a pictograph of it all right there, right there in the grotto. A pictograph of his youth and strength and juice and richness; of his young life and the engineering firm that the old man had made that had finally made him; of his beautiful wife and his beautiful daughter that the younger man had married; of his first car and first love and first money and first laugh and first cry and all the first things in his life and all the last things, all the great things and all the small things he would do in the pictograph now that the bath was done here in this perfect place, this right place of all right places.

Before the old man turned, the younger man ducked back into the boat. He poured the boiling water into two cups and made coffee as the old man swam back to the boat and came up the stern ladder. He pretended not to have seen the bath, not to have seen the prayer. Then the two men sat in the cockpit and drank the coffee and stared at the high rock walls while the younger man wished the old man could live forever, but he could not.

The Face of the Tiger

WHEN I WAS a child I seemed to be sick with a successive run of illnesses that put me close to death.

In those years many young people died from illnesses that would now be considered trivial. An ear infection could trigger a fever, cause convulsions, and kill a child in a matter of hours. That fast, and they were gone.

In northern Minnesota, where I was a child, the old church graveyards are filled with small graves, tiny graves with headstones remembering children. "Gone to the Final Rest," they read. "At Play in the Fields of the Lord."

Antibiotics were not widely used and a tiny cut, if it became infected, could easily prove fatal. I had many of those—tiny cuts, infections, and sickness. I had an attack of appendicitis on a train from Chicago to Minneapolis. I remember vomiting over the top of the seat in front of me onto a bald man's head and doubling with pain as they tried to find a doctor somewhere in one of the cars. And I would have died then, had they not got me to a small hospital and operated that night.

As they put the ether mask over my face, and the stink of the gas cut into my throat, I screamed and I saw my mother there. She had what I came to call the face of the tiger. Her eyes looked worried and tight with something I did not understand. It looked like anger, though I could not understand why she was angry at me for becoming ill, and it frightened me. I did not know that the anger was not for me but was for someone else; I did not understand that she would become the tiger and literally fight to save me.

Once when danger came in an alley near our Minneapolis apartment, I saw my mother fight, saw her become the tiger for the first time.

There were then, just as there are now, terrible, sick, depraved, and disgusting men who preyed on children and my mother warned me about them, told me the clichés about taking candy from strangers, but when the danger came it did not offer me candy.

I was in back of a small billboard, peeing in the corner it formed with a building, when suddenly the corner grew dark and there was a man. He was an older man with stubble, but he was not dirty, not a bum. He was just a man standing in the opening between the wall and the sign, and he said nothing.

His eyes were too bright and he licked his lips and fumbled with his fly. I tried to run past him but he grabbed me by the shirt and held me and I know now, I feel now how close I was to an end there. He was strong and I could not get away and there in the corner of the sign he grunted and held me and I wanted to scream and I could not even do that. I dangled like a rabbit taken by a wolf, not able to move, not able to do anything but hang and wait for whatever was coming, wait in stunned shock, and then I felt the man lurch sideways.

"You son of a bitch!" my mother screamed, her voice a rake with teeth. "You drop him, you son of a bitch, you son of a bitch. . . ."

I scrabbled free through the man's legs, but instead of running I turned and looked back because my mother had changed. She had grown and was something different then, she was no longer attacking the man to get me free, but attacking him to end him, to kill him, to kill all that he represented. She hit him again and again, knocking him down, and when he was down she kicked him in the head. He yelled, but she was almost silent, her breath coming in short snarls, and when he tried to cover his head with his hands, she found holes, openings, and she kicked him again and again with her sharp pointed shoes until she found his temple and he lay still. I do not know if she killed him. I only know that to my young eyes he looked very still, except that his fingers curled and uncurled slowly, the way a snake will move when its head is gone.

Then she stopped and leaned over him and spat on him, ripping great breaths, and she said one more time, "Not him, you son of a bitch, not my son."

She took my hand and led me home and spanked me for going behind the billboard. For days I watched her, my mother. She was not a large woman, but well built, sturdy, from farm stock, and strong from a life of working hard. Strong and straight with large breasts, immense eyes, fine teeth, and great Nordic beauty that belied her strength. I watched her, waiting for the face of the tiger to come again, fearing that she would hurt me, but it did not come again until I was dying in a hospital and I saw her with the priest.

For a time during the war I seemed to draw pneumonia like honey draws flies, and my mother took care of me. I would get a cold, it would turn into pneumonia, then get worse and turn into double pneumonia, and then after a stay in the hospital, I would recover. Then, not long after, I would fall sick again and get pneumonia.

It seemed an endless circle that would ultimately have one end, and an end came, finally, in a hospital room in Minneapolis. I cycled into a cold and then pneumonia and then double pneumonia and the doctors told my mother that I would not live. I was not there when they told her this, but I knew it was different this time because they put me in an oxygen tent and the nurses moved in silence. They looked at me through the wrinkled plastic as my breathing rasped, and my mother sat next to the bed, watching me with sadness as she held my hand beneath the tent.

Of course I did not know how sick I was. I only knew it was different this time, and I felt sad because everyone else seemed so sad.

I thought of my cousin who had died from a minor kidney infection just two months before. I had gone to his funeral where I sat between his mother and mine. I had seen his body in the casket, and I thought that that was all dying was—to be in a casket and to leave.

Now I was close to leaving, and I would drift in and out of seeing my mother through the tent, her eyes red from crying, her hand holding mine, while I heard the hiss of oxygen and the pull of my own breath. And that is when the priest came into the room.

We were no religion much, but we were not Catholic the most, and when my mother turned and saw the priest she went into a rage. He was the hospital chaplain and he had heard that a boy was dying and he came into the room to help. But my mother did not see it as that. Her eyes blazed, and she saw death.

He meant death, meant to her that I was dying, and she screamed, "You son of a bitch, not now, get out of here!"

And she swore as she leapt from the side of the bed with the same growl she had used on the man in back of the billboard. She attacked the priest with her hands open, slapping him back and back through the door and out of the room. Then she came back in, slammed the door, and looked up. The low throaty sound filled her words and she said, "Not now, you son of a bitch, not this one."

And of course she meant God. She would fight

Him, would not let Him take me, and I thought, felt, *knew* then that nothing could hurt me as long as she was over me, my tiger mother, with her low sounds and her strong arms and hands, and I saw it all through the crinkled plastic of the oxygen tent in the hospital room in Minneapolis.

Aunt Caroline

THERE WAS AN AUNT named Caroline and she was so beautiful.

Once when he was a boy and the pimples had him and he could think of nothing but his lust, once when he was that young that his mind was torn apart each time he passed Shirley Parren in the hall, once when there was nothing in the world for him but the sweet ripping agony of being hatefully too young to do any of the things that seared through his brain, once when there was not a moment of any waking day that he did not think about being driven by his lust, once when that was in him, upon him, he was sent to his Aunt Caroline's house on an errand.

He knocked on the door for a long time as it was early in the morning, early and frosty, and when she opened it, her hair was tousled with sleep, blonde and fallen, and she stood in a half-open robe with her eyes sleep-closed and the curve of her breast showing in the opening of the robe and he hated himself.

With all the intensity of his youth he hated himself. He did not know what he would find later, and still later.

Later he would find these things about himself:

He would find of himself that he could be married not once, but three times; once in the breathy loneliness of youth, once in the heady-musk-flush of lust, and once in what he thought to be love.

He would find of himself that he could feel love, or thought he could feel love, love that came from some part of him that he did not understand, where he thought all good love must come from, and he would have great difficulty separating the love from something else and would fight to do it all his life although he did not know why.

He would find of himself that he could help to make children and help to raise children and help to harm children all without meaning to, caring very much for the children but not knowing how to be indifferent and callous enough to let them go.

He would find of himself that the sweat part of it, the driven part of him that made him seek the company of women was not all that he thought it was, and was, at times, a hindrance.

He would find of himself that he was not always right, was indeed usually wrong.

He would find of himself, in the army and at some other times, that he could feel the white-hot great fear of quick-flash death, and he wanted to live forever.

He would find of himself that he was not capable of judging another person, was not capable of telling another person how to live or be, and yet spent a great deal of time inside lives other than his own.

He would find of himself that he had vanity, though he tried not to in his mind, and when his hair started to thin he tried to comb the remaining hairs over the bald spot, though he tried not to in his mind, and when a young woman walked by he held his stomach in. He wore clothes that hid his extra weight, though he tried not to in his mind. And he grew older and more vain, though he tried not to in his mind.

He would find of himself that he could make money and spend money, be successful and be a failure, and have power over other men, and let other men have power over him.

He would find of himself that he did not understand the paradox of life any better then anyone else. He would say that just when you know how to do it, the bastards take it away from you. He said it often and laughed when he said it and called it a great joke and felt it was knowledge, but he was really bewildered by it and afraid.

He would find of himself that he was not a bad person, just as he was not a good person, but only a simple man.

He would find of himself that he could live and be alone, just as he had thought he could not live and be alone but would always have to be with somebody.

He would find of himself that he was capable of tremendous folly, astounding self-destructive folly that could ruin his life and the lives of all those who were close to him, the folly of alcohol. And he believed he was not capable of one serious, well-founded thought.

He would find of himself that when he got the blood in his stool it ended all the dreams of his life.

He would find of himself that all of his ambitions, all of his dreams, all of everything that he was, or ever would be, were of no importance when he came to the end of it; all of it was without merit except as the process of living and the process was something expected of him. And he was surprised to find of himself that the knowing did not make him sad or frustrated, but instead it liberated him, opened his mind.

He would find of himself that when it was done, when he had passed blood in his stool, and the doctors began to take what he was away, take what he had made away, take even the process away, when the chemical treatments were tried and there was not a way to make the process work, he found that there was serenity in it.

He would find of himself that when it was done and there could be no more, he did not feel fear. Or perhaps it was a controlled fear, and it did not make him tighten and die inside as did the other fear, the fear that came with men trying to kill men.

He would find of himself in the end that he was a
man, only a man, and as such he did not need to hate
himself nor love himself, but just be a man in the
world. And he would find of himself, finally, that he
knew nothing of himself just as others knew nothing
of him and he would end in ignorance just as he
began in ignorance.

But all of this was later, later as he wore into his life
and found it and lost it; all of it was later and later
during the living of it, and none of it was there when
he was sent on the errand and saw his Aunt Caroline
standing in the cold morning door with a half open
robe and the curve of her breast and the tumbling
blonde hair falling down the sides of her head.

All he could think then was how he hated himself
for his thoughts. And when he went out one night
with Shirley Parren, and they parked at Black Hill, he
thought of his Aunt Caroline again. But as the time
went and the darkness went, he did not think of her
anymore, and he would not think of her again until
he had blood in his stool and they could do nothing
for him.

The Soldier

WHEN HE WAS DONE for the day he went back to the barracks, the tall, sand-colored barracks that dated back to the old cavalry days. He walked past old Fort Bliss where once there had been horses tied and where the old gatling gun still sat in hot, dusty memory of how it had been when they fought the Apaches there. He walked back to the barracks and took off his khakis and hung them in his locker. He put on his civvies and changed from low-quarter shoes into cowboy boots and put on a western shirt. And then he went out the main gate with his overnight pass and he crossed over the bridge into Jaurez.

But he was, of course, still a soldier.

With all that, looking in the mirror in his locker and then in the large mirror in the squad room as he left the barracks, he could see that he was still a soldier. He had a short haircut and a too-trimmed mustache and side-burns and a straight back and upright carriage and he could see he was still a soldier and everybody else could see it as well.

When he crossed the bridge into Mexico, the screaming children, the border children under the bridge could tell what he was:

"G.I!" They shouted. "Throw money here! Throw money here!"

He threw them quarters and nickels. Some of the children had cardboard cones on the ends of sticks to catch the money, but if they missed they jumped into the ugly brown water and fought with their hands on the bottom in the mud and broken glass to find the money, the small money. And if a smaller child came up with the money, a larger child would beat him and take it, the small money.

On the glittering, loud, and crowded strip beyond the bridge they could tell what he was:

"G.I.! G.I.! You want my sister? She's a virgin! She's a virgin! Only five dollar! Take my sister!"

There had been a time, when he first came into the army, that he had taken one of their "sisters" to a small room and put some money on the dresser, a time when he had gone through the motions that meant nothing, had gone faster and faster until the end. He had told his sergeant it made him feel like a man, but it did not. It did not make him feel anything except disgust and anger at his own weakness and he had not done it again. He would not do it again.

When he got to the club called the Two-by-Six he went in and exchanged the street noise for the club noise inside. There were strippers in the Two-by-Six and sometimes they danced well. They were not for sale, but he came there for Maria. He had met Maria when he first came back from duty and he thought Maria might even be her real name, though it did not matter. Many of them—perhaps all of them—were named Maria, and in his fashion, in the tired drunk fashion of what he was he loved her. When Maria was done dancing, and when the soldier had had enough tequila to be mildly drunk, they would leave together and go to the Rio Brava Hotel. It was down by the railroad tracks, near the bullring. It was the same hotel, they had told him, that Pancho Villa had attacked when he took Jaurez, and he knew it was true because he could see the bullet holes and grooves in the outside walls. And the soldier knew that bullets, of all things, didn't lie; bullets had given him many truths and not once a lie.

He and Maria would go to the Rio Brava Hotel where they would undress and he would notice the small marks on her stomach and nipples, marks that told him that she had been pregnant, though he never asked about that. They would make love in the old bed and then he would leave, just before dawn, to return to the barracks. He would take the bus back to the sand-colored barracks to make the morning roll call, because he was, after all of it, a soldier.

But on this night there was a young girl in the Two-by-Six, young and coltish, working the tables to get drink money—drinking colored water and charging the full price—and she came to him and sat in his lap and groped him and asked him to buy her a drink. He said no, politely at first, then with more force when she insisted, and finally he pushed her away and the table fell to one side.

It was a simple thing, but the manager rushed out from behind the bar and ordered her to leave, firing her in Spanish. And to the soldier it sounded the same as someone being fired in English.

The young girl begged the manager to let her stay, pleading with dark eyes and the movement of the hips that meant so much, but the manager shook his head. And then she knew it was done. She turned to the soldier and he saw a great fear. He saw terror in her eyes as she spat a curse at him, but he did not understand the words. He watched her retreat with the jerky movement of someone who is so afraid they cannot walk correctly.

When she was gone, he turned to the man at the bar. "Why does she have such fear?" the soldier asked.

"She is from out on the edge of town," said the man at the bar, "out in the mud huts. She must go back out there and live. She is no good here. But they do not last long out there—not girls like that—and she knows it."

"But for a table—all she did was tip the table."

"No. She was trouble. Too pushy with the drinks,

and wanting to go upstairs too soon before they had bought enough. She was wrong for it."

"Christ, man. She's just a kid. . . ."

But the manager turned away and instructed the waiter to bring the soldier a fresh tequila. Then the brass music started and Maria came out on the runway and the soldier did not think of the girl again until he was riding the bus back to Fort Bliss in the gray light of the early morning. And then the thought came and went with the flare of his lighter when he lit his cigarette, just the quick thought of the girl and her jerky fear movement. He had had that fear once, fear just as that, and he hoped he would never have it again.

The Liberty Ship

I STILL HAVE the pictures, gray and black and small, but they don't show it as I remember it, the way I saw it from the rail of the Liberty Ship, as I watched the woman trying to save her baby.

In 1946 I was seven years old and my father was Army in the Pacific—that's how we said it, he was Army in the Pacific—stationed in the Philippines, and with the war done my mother and I were going to live with him. We rode trains for a week across deserts and up the coast to San Francisco where we were to board the Liberty Ship and sail for three more weeks to get to Manila.

But two days before the ship was to sail I came down with the chickenpox. It was illegal for anyone with a communicable disease to leave the country, so my mother talked to the captain of the ship and I was smuggled on board one night wrapped in a blanket. I was hidden below deck in a cabin with no porthole and told I could not leave until the pox had cleared up.

It was little better than a cell, but because many of the soldiers and sailors on the ship heard about me and because they liked children—and, perhaps, because my mother was a beautiful woman—they brought me comic books and candy bars. To this day I cannot open a Hershey bar without hearing the hum of the ship's engines and smelling the fumes from the steel and the paint and the diesel.

Every third day the captain would come with my mother and put on white gloves and inspect my cabin, rubbing his finger over the door to look for dust. He terrified me so that I spent most of my time cleaning the cabin. Hour after hour, I scrubbed with a rag they gave me, dampened in a small metal sink bolted to the bulkhead next to a seatless toilet, scrubbed until

I thought it was clean.

And always the white glove came away from the wall or bunk or shelf dirty and he would frown down on me and shake his head and say, "Not good enough. Not good enough at all."

It may have been a joke, because my mother was with him and smiled once or twice, but he represented all the power of the sea and ships and God to me. I hated him for his inspections then, and I still hate him. I was down in a metal hole, having my meals slid to me on a tray as if I were a leper, never seeing the sky or the sun, and all the time I was scrubbing and cleaning and worrying about the next inspection, living in horror of it, knowing that it would not be good enough. Day after day, the weeks passed with just the hum of the ships engines.

When we stopped in Hawaii, I was not allowed out. And then we sailed again.

Sailing toward the woman and her baby.

One day, when the pox seemed almost gone in the mirror above the sink, the hatch slammed open and my mother stood there breathless gasping, "Come quick. A plane is going to crash!"

She turned and ran and as I started to follow her I saw my camera, a little Brownie box, and I grabbed it. I had trouble keeping up with her. Up through the companionways, up through the maze of ladders, up from the bowels of the ship we climbed until we plunged, suddenly, into the bright sun on deck where I squinted at the new light, squinted and there it was, the airplane coming down.

The plane was a four-engine transport, its aluminum skin shining in the sun against the brilliant blue of the Pacific. The two left engines looked frozen, the propellors still, and the two right ones were turning slowly. The plane was coming down toward the ship. It seemed to flare at last like a big bird, a huge bird settling gently, slowly down to the water. But it wasn't so slow and it wasn't gentle at all.

When it hit the waves, not a quarter mile from the ship, it threw up a blinding curtain of water as if it had hit a liquid wall. The plane skipped for a distance, a little sideways, and came to rest, finally, not two hundred yards from the ship.

It began to sink immediately. The fuselage sank first, but the wings seemed to float longer. When the wings were almost completely awash, in a matter of seconds, the plane seemed to hang up, half sunk, and hesitate. Suddenly, the doors opened and people began jumping out into the water. Many of them were women holding children. Then I heard, as the lifeboats from the ship were being lowered, that it was a flight of military dependents—wives and children of servicemen—on their way overseas to be with their families. Just like my mother and me.

All I saw was the blue of the water, the whitecaps, the hot sun, and the ship. I saw the plane sinking slowly, its passengers leaping into the waves. I saw the lifeboats breaking free from the davits and firing their engines to cross to the plane. I was taking pictures as fast as I could, cranking the film until the next number showed in the red window, then raising it to shoot again. It all seemed a scene from a movie—not real, just an adventure. It was a grand adventure just for me, for my camera.

And then the sharks found them

We could not see the sharks from the ship—the sharks that always follow the ships for the garbage thrown over the stern. But we could hear the people scream when the sharks hit them, and we could see the effect of them. Young people went down like fishing bobbers, jerked once or twice, then a scream, and then they went under. My mother tried to cover my eyes but I kept peeking through, taking more pictures. I can remember the screams now, I remember the screams and the jerking at the small bodies as they went down. Once, twice, and down. Again and again.

But most, most I can remember the mother. She had a baby in her hands and she was holding it up, out of the water. She tried to put it up on the wing of the plane, but the child kept sliding off. She would push it back up again, but again it would slide off into the water. And she was pushing like that when the sharks found her. They hit her in the legs, slamming her and taking their bites. She kept pushing the baby up onto the wing and the sharks kept hitting her, jerking her down as she fought to save her child, her gentle hands holding the baby up as the sharks jerked her back and down until she was gone. Then the baby slid off the wing, and they had the baby, too. The sharks had the mother and the baby when the ship's boats finally reached the plane and started pulling the people out of the water.

I have the pictures somewhere, gray and black and small, and they don't show it as I remember it: all blues and sun and screams. They don't show the mother holding her baby up, up away from the sharks until nothing was left. But I still have the pictures somewhere.

The Library

I FIRST STARTED seriously going to the library to work after I left Hollywood and moved to a cabin in the north woods. Leaving Hollywood was necessary because it was ugly then, and perhaps it still is. It was ugly in the way it made everything beautiful. It had gotten inside of me and damaged me in the way that everything beautiful can damage a person. It made me greedy for more and more of whatever it was that was destroying me, and it fed me to myself until I was nearly consumed. So I ran—as others had run, I suppose—until I found a cheap cabin in the northern woods of Minnesota. And there I thought I would sit and write grand things.

But the leap was too vast. From the parties of Hollywood where we told each other how brilliant we were, to the woods, the silent woods where you could tell nobody anything but had to prove it to yourself. That was too great a jump. I became afraid. Afraid that I was only meant for Hollywood, afraid that I had no substance, and I reached out for something that could help me end the fear.

In the nearby town of Poplar there was an old library. It still had the shiny hardwood shelves and the hardwood card catalog and a librarian named Pearl who knew books, knew the quality of books, and one day I found myself there, in the library, lost. I was looking for something to read, but looking for more, too.

Much more.

I needed to bridge the gap from where I'd been, and I knew the library would help. The quiet of the library would help.

It was a high building made of brick. It had large windows with arched tops and molded decorations around the sides, and the small panes that made me think of French windows. Inside, the windows went almost to the ceiling, and the walls were a faded yellow. When the sun streamed in, it was as if the room were bathed in gold, dusty gold with little motes riding down the beams of light to fall on the round oak tables where you could sit and read.

I had forgotten how to sit and read. In the crush of what I had been doing there had not been time to enjoy reading. But I found that in the library I could sit, just sit, and read. And it was not long after I learned to read again that I first met the ladies.

The ladies.

In the early fall I had started to come to the library three or four days a week to read. Then the weather turned off, as they say here, turned off colder and still colder until there was ice in the water pitcher in my cabin each morning. After two weeks of such cold, the town lake was frozen and I walked through the steam of my breath when I moved outside. And while there was great beauty in the cold, there was discomfort as well. Frozen fingers and ears, parts that tingled with pain when I came into a warm room. Fogged glasses. Tight breath. No snow yet, but the promise was there. The hard promise of winter.

On one of those mornings I walked the two miles to the library. I stopped just inside the door to clear my glasses, and when I put them back on, the ladies were there.

There were eight of them that first time. Later there were as many as fifteen, but never fewer than eight that winter. In the sunlight that fell through the small window panes sat eight gray-haired women. They wore shawls and they sat around two tables drawn together so they could all be in one group, and they were crocheting—fine lace, doilies, a bed-spread, and perhaps a tablecloth. Fingers thin with large joints, and the graceful swing-hook, swing-hook of the crochet hooks.

I tried not to stare. They were so beautiful. The way they sat in the golden light with their gray hair pulled back in tight buns or in close curls, their hands moving with the hooks, the thread flying through and making lace, all in the light, the dusty light—I had to look away to keep from staring.

"Are you all right?" Pearl, at the desk just inside the door, had seen me stop.

"Fine," I said. "It's just the ladies, all sitting that way. They look like a painting, an old painting. It made me pause."

Pearl started to say something, but a man came into the library and she turned to take his books. I went into the reading room with my notebook. The ladies had taken the table where I usually worked. I put my notebook at another one near the magazines and sat to work, but my pencil was broken, and I went to the sharpener at the front.

Pearl had finished with the man and was checking his books.

"Sometimes they break the backs," she said, as I came to the desk. "It's not that they mean to, of course, but sometimes they break the backs. I always check them."

I nodded. I looked at the women again.

"They work so hard at crocheting," I said. "Who are they, some kind of ladies' club?"

Pearl smiled. A sad smile, a quiet library sad smile, and she shook her head slowly.

"No," she said. "They can't afford to heat their homes, so they turn off their heaters and come here during the day to save fuel."

Ahh, I thought. Ahh, here is a savage thing, a viciously savage thing to have so much beauty around it. They were casualties, as I was, and that made them suddenly close to me. I thought for a moment that I should talk to them but knew that would be wrong. I knew instead that I should listen to them and so I went back to the table and sat as near as I could.

And I listened.

I'm not sure what I expected. Maybe anger, anger that they had to stay out of their homes. Maybe wisdom. Maybe knowledge. Maybe hope. When I listened, I got some of all of it. But mostly, mostly they talked the stories of their lives.

There was song in the way they talked and song in what they said. And after a time, after days and weeks of sitting there listening to them, I heard the song more than I heard the words.

My Emmit, now, he had big hands.
My land, they were so big he could hold a bird
with a broken wing.
Hold it so you couldn't see anything.
Not a feather.
And the bird never hurt, never hurt a bit.

When we first came north we built a granary.
All of wood.
And we slept upstairs.
Then a barn.
And we slept upstairs.
Finally we made a house, a home.
All of wood. And so tight the wind
had to fight to find a hole.

Talk of wedding dresses!
Mine had ruffles all down the back,
Like a waterfall. And a silk bodice.
With a white veil. A white veil.
I still have the veil somewhere.

When my Clyde came to be married
he was in a suit so black and stiff
he looked like a stove pipe.
But he worked hard.
And I loved him.

We didn't make a crop for six years,
in the depression.
It almost broke my Will.
Almost broke him.
And I don't care if I never
see another bean.

We burned out twice.
The first time it was only the house.
And the barn. And some chickens.
But the second time was worse.
We lost the baby then.
Little Bets.
Chimney fire both times.
But the second time was worse.

My first husband was John.
We had a year
and two months
and three days.
Then they came and took him.
The War took him.
I didn't even get the body.

My Jim, he never quit joking.
Not even at the end,
when his hair was gone
from the treatment.
He told everybody it was a joke,
he was studying to be a clown.

When I got married, my mother cried,
and gave me a saucepan,
and some dishes.
It was all she had to give me,
tears and dishes.

At first when they came and I sat and listened to them talk, listened to them sing, I had great pity for them. I thought they were done, as I thought I was done. And when I had pity for them, I also had pity for myself, because those women were me, were talking about me.

But then I saw them as they really were, thought of them not as something to be pitied, but something to respect. They were something to respect, those ladies, those women who could not heat their homes. They were lionesses, old lionesses who had lived and hunted and been all that they wanted to be and now sat in the golden sun and rested and compared lives. Lionesses who had earned the right to rest, to rest in the dusty sun in the library. And when one would quit coming and I would find that she had died, I felt sad at the loss but respected that, too.

And that is how I came to work seriously in the library.